Letters to Liz: Zoe's Letter

Mary Hooper knows more than most people what makes a good story – she's had over six hundred published in teenage and women's magazines such as *J17*, and is the highly regarded author of over fifty titles for young people, including *Best Friends, Worst Luck*; *Mad About the Boy*; *The Boyfriend Trap*; and the Letters to Liz series. She recently won the 2000 North-east Book Award for her teenage novel, *Megan*. Mary has two grown-up children, Rowan and Gemma, and lives in an old cottage in Hampshire.

Books by the same author

Amber's Letter
Jo's Letter
Nicki's Letter
Best Friends, Worst Luck
The Boyfriend Trap
Mad About the Boy
The Peculiar Power of Tabitha Brown

Letters to Liz:
Zoe's Letter

Mary Hooper

WALKER BOOKS
AND SUBSIDIARIES

LONDON • BOSTON • SYDNEY

First published 2002 by Walker Books Ltd
87 Vauxhall Walk, London SE11 5HJ

2 4 6 8 10 9 7 5 3 1

Text © 2002 Mary Hooper
Cover illustration © 2002 Rian Hughes
Cover design by Rian Hughes at Device

The right of Mary Hooper to be identified as author
of this work has been asserted by her in accordance
with the Copyright, Designs and Patents Act 1988

This book has been typeset in ITC Highlander Book

Printed and bound in Great Britain by The Guernsey Press Co. Ltd

British Library Cataloguing in Publication Data:
a catalogue record for this book
is available from the British Library

ISBN 0-7445-9003-5

Chapter One

Dear Liz,

I've never written to an agony aunt before. In fact, I've always thought that people who write to magazines with their problems are pretty sad. This is something that I just can't tell my friends, though. It's a really big problem and it seems to have taken over my life. It's about a boy. Of course, it mostly is when girls are writing to you, but I'll tell you now that it's not like me to get so hooked on a boy that I can't think straight.

It all started two nights ago, at the skating rink...

I put down my pen and closed my eyes. I was going to write the letter in rough first, and then type it out afterwards, but I wanted to sort things out in my head before I started.

We – me, Amber, Jo and Nicki – had gone skating, just for something to do, really. The four of us are really good friends. We've been going round together for ages now, since about the second year of primary school, although my mum was all set to break us up when I was twelve because she didn't want me to go on to the local comprehensive with them. She's a bit like that – a real snob – and she was going to send me off to some posh boarding school. I kicked up a fuss about leaving the others, though – said I would run away – and in the end she gave in and let me stay.

Anyway, we'd decided to go ice-skating, just to make a change from drinking Cokes in Beany's or going down the square to see who was hanging out. Also, Jo had got these vouchers that gave two-for-one entry to the rink, so we thought we might as well give it a go.

We didn't go down there to try and meet boys, but if there were any around that we hadn't seen before (you can always hope) then that would be a bonus. Mind you, Amber wasn't really interested in meeting anyone, because she had Mac. Mac has recently come to our school from Scotland. He's well fit, with a gorgeous body and a Highlander accent so strong you could cut porridge with it. At first we'd laughed at the way he spoke, and the boys had taken the mick out of him, but actually all of us girls reckoned his accent was gorgeous. I could have listened to it all day.

So anyway, we got to the rink, hired our skates and sat around lacing them up, trying on each other's and changing them at the counter until we were satisfied they fitted OK. We were a bit giggly and nervous. I mean, we'd all been roller-blading before so we weren't going to be totally useless, but no one likes to look a complete dork, do they?

It was the first time I'd been ice-skating there – it was sort of old-fashioned with funny big globe lights and glittery disco balls. The rink itself was huge and echoey, and a frosty sort of mist hung over the ice.

We pulled each other round, pushed each other over and shrieked and giggled as we went round the rink a few times, mostly holding onto the edge. Then we hobbled along to the bar, still on our blades, to get a Coke.

We started talking about boys, of course, and whether there was anyone there we liked the look of. Jo, who isn't usually into boys as much as the rest of us, said she really fancied the guy who'd given out the boots, and Amber said she couldn't think about anyone else because she was completely mad about Mac. She said she was never going to fancy anyone else as long as she lived.

Course, we all screeched with laughter at this.

"I *won't*," Amber said. She's got red-gold hair and she tucked a strand of it behind one ear and squeezed her eyes up tightly. "He's so ... so utterly gorgeous in every way."

"He's just a bloke!" I said. "How can he be?"

The other two laughed but Amber was quite insistent. "If you knew him like I do you'd think the same," she said. "He's got a way of really listening to you. He's so understanding. He always wants to know what I've been doing and what I think about and all that. And he's thoughtful."

"Thoughtful?" I said. "That's a new one!"

"I've never heard any of the blokes we've been out with called thoughtful before," Nicki said.

"Exactly," Amber went on. "Mac really likes girls. He knows what makes them tick."

Well, we all laughed again but it got me thinking. Why couldn't I get a boy like that? Someone *thoughtful.* Someone who knew how to treat a girl. The ones I got were usually good-looking, flash jack-the-lads, and could never be called thoughtful by any stretch of the imagination. And if they were, it was only for one reason. Like they'd "thoughtfully" ask you round to their house to copy a CD for you, and then you'd find it just so happened that their parents were out, and then they'd "thoughtfully" ask you if you wanted to watch a video, and they'd "thoughtfully" turn the lights down, and – well, you get the picture.

We all finished our drinks and then went back on the rink. Holding onto each other and grabbing at the sides for support, we actually managed to go round a few times without falling over.

We sat down again and Nicki said she'd twisted her ankle a bit. We were just discussing whether we could manage another drink or should just go home, when there was a "Hey!" from the other side of the rink and who should appear but Mac, waving wildly at us. He was with Sam, a boy I'd gone out with a couple of times in the distant past.

They came onto the ice and speed-skated over, curling round to a halt in front of us in the way that boys do, spraying up ice.

"Not bad!" Amber said. She was so happy to see him. I thought to myself that when she'd packed in her last boyfriend – some creep called Jamie – it was the best thing she'd ever done.

"I practised in the Highlands," Mac said. "You can

skate down mountains there."

"You come from Glasgow," I said. "They haven't got mountains."

"OK then," he grinned at me. "It's just my natural grace and skill."

"Yeah, right," I said.

Sam spoke up. "So you got the half-price vouchers too?"

We all nodded.

"We've been here an hour or so. My feet are freezing!" Amber said. "We were just thinking about going home."

"Och, do a couple of rounds with me before you go," Mac said.

Amber started pulling her gloves on again.

"OK. But promise you won't go too fast?"

"Would I do that?"

He led her off onto the ice and Sam took Jo for a spin round at the same time. I'd had enough, really, so I said I'd sit with Nicki while she wiggled her ankle to get it back to normal.

I watched Mac and Amber on the ice; he had his arm around her, pulling her close, and every so often she'd laugh up at him or give a squeal of enjoyment. Lucky old Amber, I thought, to have that sort of a relationship with someone. I had a boyfriend too – a guy called Paul who was in the year above us – but it wasn't going anywhere. He was just someone to hang around with, like everyone else I'd ever been out with, really.

Mac and Amber went round the rink twice and

then she arrived, puffing, back beside me. "It's much better when you're with someone who knows what they're doing," she said. "It was really good fun."

Mac looked at me and held out his hand. "Want some of that really good fun, Zoe?" he said in his gorgeous accent, and for a moment I just sat there, staring up at him, struck dumb and feeling sort of hypnotized.

That's really odd for me, because – well, I'm not being big-headed but I've got very long blonde hair and I got boobs quite early on, so I've never exactly been hard-up for boys. They're like buses, I always say – there'll be another one along in a minute.

When Mac said that, though, and looked at me, I felt a shiver run all over me. Why hadn't I noticed him before? This guy was something else...

So, we just went around the rink together and had a laugh, but for the rest of the evening I just felt like I was in a sort of trance. All I could think of, all I could see, was Mac. He was all around me, all over me ... I could still feel his fingers on my arm.

I picked up my pen again – I hadn't got very far with the letter.

Liz, nothing happened except he looked at me, spoke my name and took me once around the ice rink, but it's just made me feel absolutely weird. I can't stop thinking about him...

I put the pad away. Thinking was OK, but trying to

write the things that I felt was too difficult. How could you translate feelings into words?

Mac. I conjured him up in my head, and tried saying my name aloud the way he said it: it sounded like Zoo-ey.

Mac. I was mad about him. And he was going out with Amber.

Chapter Two

When I got in from ice-skating, Mum was out. Of course. She was at some business dinner or other and eventually arrived home in a taxi at midnight.

The other girls think I'm dead lucky having a mum who's never there. Nicki especially (her mum is a right nag) is always going on about how jammy I am. OK, it's good in a way, but I get fed up with coming home in the evenings and never finding anyone in, never having anyone to talk to. I don't say much to the other three about this because I know they'd give anything to live the way I do – what with my freedom and my allowance and our big house – but it's not really what I want. What I want is a mum who's there when I need her.

Mum not only works late, but she goes away on trips quite a lot – to Europe and the USA. When she's away for a couple of nights I have to go to my gran's house, or my aunt's, and that's a right drag. Oh, I know Mum earns a colossal amount of money and I can have anything I want, but after a while that stops being so important. I mean, there are other things in life besides earning money the whole time. When I'm married with a baby, I'm not going to work. Or if I do, I'll make sure I have time for my kids. I'll put them first.

*   *   *

A few nights later, on a Friday, the four of us met at my house and then we went down to the square, where a whole lot of kids from school hang out. Mac was there, and Paul, and I had an opportunity to compare them.

Paul's a year older than Mac and is quite a loud sort of person. I mean, he's one of those guys who're always taking the mick out of people, or imitating them, laughing at them and making everyone else crack up. Don't get me wrong, he's OK as a person, but there's not a lot *to* him. I mean, you couldn't ever imagine telling him you had a problem and then the two of you sitting down quietly and talking about it.

He's all right, though. He's the sort of boy I usually go out with. I was hoping that when I saw him next to Mac, the funny feelings I had about Mac would disappear and I'd go back to normal.

It didn't happen like that, though...

By the Friday I'd worked myself into a dreamy can't sleep/can't eat state. Amber, Jo and Nicki knew nothing about this, of course. Apart from it being wrong to get a crush on your friend's boyfriend, I've got this reputation, you see. I'm the main girl, the do anything one who gets any boy she wants. Once you've got a reputation as the leader of the pack, it's hard to shake it off. Me? So hung-up about a boy that I couldn't sleep? They'd never believe it!

By eight o'clock in the square, I'd done all the comparing I was going to do. Paul was nothing next to Mac. A form of plant life. As soon as I could decently dump him, I was going to, whether anything

23

came of this thing with Mac or not.

Mac came over and chatted to us a few times and I acted just the same as usual — teasing him about some football game, saying his choice of music was dire. He kept catching my eye and once or twice I knew he was staring at me, but I didn't react at all. I didn't want Amber to have the slightest suspicion that I fancied him. OK, all's fair in love and war, but my friends are really important to me and until I was sure that he fancied me in return, I wasn't going to mess things up between them. I'd never made a play for a friend's boyfriend before.

A big group had formed from our school — there were about twenty of us. We'd all been fooling around and then Mac suddenly walked off, saying he was going to get something to eat from the burger van on the bridge. It felt like he looked at me as he said it, and there was an unspoken message in his eyes: *Come along too...*

Or was it all just my imagination?

I decided to take a chance. About thirty seconds later I left the others and went after him, shouting back that I was going to get some chips.

Maybe, I thought as I went towards the bridge, it's all just a fantasy. Maybe he hasn't been giving me the eye. If I just chat to him now, maybe it'll be a perfectly ordinary conversation and I'll stop thinking there's something going on between us and everything can go back to normal.

I joined some others in the queue. I was two

behind Mac and I stared at the back of his head, thinking it was the most gorgeous head I'd ever seen in my life. Suddenly, though, as if he knew I was there, he turned and caught me staring. He smiled, and slipped out of the queue to stand beside me.

"I thought you might come," he said.

I shrugged, trying to act casual. "Just wanted some chips. I'm starving."

"Is that the only reason?" he said, looking down at me.

I could feel my heart pounding. His eyes looked into mine – they were a true, almost emerald, green – and he said, "I think we both know why we've come up here."

When he said that, my knees turned to jelly.

He was so *sure* of himself. And so right. I forgot all my smart, flirty remarks in reply, forgot that I was usually the one to pick who to go out with. Standing with him, I became the short-haired, flat-chested and tongue-tied kid I used to be.

"Don't we know?" he asked again.

"Y ... yes," I stammered.

"So what are we going to do about it?"

I shook my head silently, and he put his hand on my shoulder and just rubbed it gently with the palm of his hand.

I swallowed. There was a lump as big as an apple in my throat, and my mouth had gone dry.

"You and me," he said. "You feel it too, don't you, Zoe? We could be sensational together..."

Chapter Three

The next morning I tried again with the letter to Liz.
A little bit more writing, a little bit more of the story.

He's hardly said anything to me, Liz. We haven't
kissed yet, but I know when we do it's going to be
amazing. The thing is, what shall I do about Amber?
Do you think I should tell her what's going on? Or shall
I go out with him first and make sure that this whole
thing, everything I'm feeling, is true?

I closed my eyes. This was happening all the time now; whenever I was on my own, I'd drift off into a dream world. This was unheard of for me. *Weird*. I didn't *do* soppy about boys.

I forced myself to look at my letter again. I'd read somewhere that problem pages received thousands of letters a week. How come, though? Why didn't people talk to their friends or their parents about their problems? It was weird, writing to someone you didn't know. Telling someone all the things that no one else knew. OK, so in my case I could hardly speak to Amber, but why couldn't I talk to my mum? That's what mums were supposed to be there for.

I heard her downstairs, clattering around. It was Saturday morning and she was giving a party that

afternoon – "just a little lunch for some new clients"
she'd said. I'd be expected to be there for the start of
it, handing round drinks and cashew nuts, but then
I'd have to clear off while they talked business.

I closed the pad I'd been writing on and put it in
my drawer. Now Mum was actually at home I ought
to make use of her. Instead of writing to someone
I didn't know, I'd go downstairs and ask her what
I should do.

She was standing at the sink in the utility room
with a big pile of flowers in front of her on the
draining board. And I mean a *big* pile. Like about ten
bunches.

"I ordered these from the florist yesterday," she
said. "I've just got to sort them out. Get me some

vases, darling, will you?"

I looked at her. It was still quite early but already she had on her full make-up, and her hair was smooth and glossy, as if she'd just come out of the salon. She always looked good, actually – always had immaculate hair, clothes and make-up, right down to her fingernails.

I found the vases and took them to her. She glanced at me. "You look a bit rough round the edges, darling. Are you sleeping all right?"

I nodded. "OK-ish. Sort of." That was a signal, really. I wanted her to ask me why I was only *sort of* sleeping.

She didn't, though. "Are those all the vases we've got?" she said. "Isn't there a huge – really gigantic – one?"

I went into the kitchen to look and came back with it. She was chopping the ends off flowers, sorting them into groups of colours. "How's the romance?" she suddenly asked.

"What romance?"

"Lloyd, isn't it? Isn't it Lloyd you're going out with? Or was that last week?"

"It's Paul, actually," I said, "but thanks for taking an interest."

She laughed. "I would take an interest but you have such a fast turnover. No sooner do I get used to a Jon than you start going out with a Michael."

She stroked my hair. "And quite right too, darling. Why shouldn't you play the field? You've got a lovely face and a gorgeous figure, you can have your pick of boys. You're far too good for those layabouts you hang around with."

I shied away from her hand stroking me and stood beside her, wondering how to start. "There's this boy I really like," I said.

"One of the layabouts?"

I sighed. "No. And they're not all *layabouts*, as you put it."

"Pass me that sharp knife there, darling," she said.

"This is someone who's just moved here from Scotland," I said. "He ... he's a really nice guy. Interesting. There's something special about him."

"There always is at first," she said. She stood back and looked at the display of flowers she'd made.

"It's top-heavy..."

"The thing is," I persevered, "he's going out with Amber."

"Oh. Well, that's just too bad, isn't it," she said. "Given a choice, he's bound to prefer you." She looked at the flowers again and gave a sigh. "Far too much pink."

"But I don't know what to do, Mum! I don't know whether to go after him, and I don't know if I should say something to Amber. I really do like him a lot."

There was a long pause while she studied the flowers again, took something out, put something else in. "I don't know," she said, shaking her head.

"What – you don't know about telling Amber, or you don't know whether I should go after him?"

"Neither," she said vaguely. "And I don't know if I should scrap this and start all over again."

"Oh, thanks a lot!" I said, and I turned on my heel and went out, slamming the door behind me. For all the good she was when she *was* at home, she might as well go to work and stay there.

I tried to write some more of the letter to Liz but I didn't know what to say. There was loads I could have written, but it was all feelings – fluffy stuff – hard to put into words. What it boiled down to was that I was mad about someone who was going out with one of my best friends. And that was all there was to it.

I stared at the writing paper for ages, doodling on it, thinking of Mac, and then I put it away.

Later, after Mum's guests had gone, Amber, Jo and Nicki came round. We finished off a pile of cold chicken and some chocolate cake, and did a quiz that was in that week's *Sue CQ*. It was called "How Deep Is Your Friendship?"

Uncomfortably enough, one of the questions was: "You reckon your best mate's boyfriend is really fit. If he started flirting with you, what would you do?"

The options were: 1. Tell him to get lost and avoid him in future; 2. Tell your friend; 3. Wait until they break up naturally, and then go for it; 4. All's fair when it comes to boys – grab him while you've got the chance!

Everyone – Jo, Nicki and Amber – put number 1. I said number 3, and I'd have liked to put number 4 but I knew they'd think I was a right cow if I did.

When we were adding up the scores later – and apart from that one, we all had more or less the same answers – the result said we were all really good friends to each other. "Boys may come and boys may go," it said, "but friendship can last a whole lot longer. Remember that and you won't go far wrong."

When Jo read that out, we all said "Aaaah!" and hugged each other. Nicki said she thought it was great that we'd all been such good mates for so long, and Amber said she couldn't possibly manage without us and she was going to make us all friendship bracelets.

I just smiled and didn't say anything.

Chapter Four

"We can't," I said to Mac huskily. "We mustn't."

Mac had hold of my shoulders. "Mustn't kiss each other?" he asked. "When we both know it's what we want most in the world?"

"You're going out with Amber..." I said. Mac was holding me gently and I was struggling – but not too hard – to get out of his grasp.

It was odd how we'd found ourselves alone together. I'd had to stay late at school to see one of the teachers about a lost book and Amber, Jo and

Nicki had gone on without me. Mac had stayed for some sports thing and he'd missed the school bus. So it was a complete coincidence – or fate – that we'd come out of school at round about the same time and happened to meet while taking the short cut through the estate.

Fate. You couldn't do anything about that, could you? If you were meant to be with someone, then that was it.

Mac and I had walked across the green together, and then sat down on one of the benches and started chatting. One thing led to another and he put his arm round me, and I rested my head on his shoulder. We were shaded by trees and the sun was casting long shadows on the grass, and soon Mac had nudged up my face so that our lips were just centimetres apart. I knew he was going to kiss me and it seemed the most natural thing in the world that he should. But...

"I can't ... Amber's my friend," I murmured, but even as I spoke I was lifting my face even closer so that he only had to move his head a fraction. And then his lips were on mine in the most perfect kiss ever.

I kept my eyes closed when it ended. I know it sounds corny but I actually felt as if I was floating. It was the most incredible sensation and I didn't want it to stop.

"Wow..." he said softly. "Some kiss. Now do you believe me? About us?"

I nodded.

"We ... could ... be ... amazing ... together," he said, giving me little kisses between each word.

My mind spun. I didn't know what to say. What did he actually mean? I *thought* I knew – he was talking about taking things further. The next stage.

Had he and Amber...? I wasn't sure. We all brag about what we've done, but a lot of it is just for effect. To sound good in front of your mates.

"Hang on," I said. "You're going a bit too fast for me. And don't forget you're still going out with Amber."

He shook his head. "Me and Amber – it doesn't mean anything," he said. "I realize now that it was a mistake to start seeing her in the first place." He stroked my hair. "Besides, I only went out with her because you weren't available. I just wanted to get closer to you."

I held my breath, moved by that confession. It was really romantic – the most romantic thing anyone had ever said to me. "So will you..." I bit my lip. "Are you going to dump her, then?"

"Sure I am," he said. "But she's a nice girl and I don't want to be a complete jerk. She's got this family wedding at the end of the month she's asked me to go to. I can't just leave her in the lurch."

I nodded slowly. I knew all about the wedding and how excited Amber was because Mac was going with her. "So after the wedding, will you...?"

"Besides," he interrupted, "you're going out with someone as well."

"Paul," I said.

"Are you thinking of two-timing him?"

I shook my head. "I'll tell him it's over. Anyway, it's just a casual thing. He's not..." I didn't say any more. *He's not mad about me like Amber is about you,* I wanted to say.

"But in the meantime I really want to see you, Zoe. Be with you. Take you somewhere special." He ran his hand down my arm, making me shiver. "We could go into town and have a romantic meal. It would be to celebrate us finding each other."

"I don't know," I said, but even as I was saying it I was thinking about how to do my hair and what to wear. I was thinking about sitting at some candlelit table opposite Mac, and of us looking into each other's eyes all through the meal. I'd never had that sort of a date with a boy.

"Come on," he said. "You know you want to. Let me ring you next week. Give me your number."

I gave it to him. Of course I did.

"OK, I'll book something. Keep Saturday night free, right?"

"Right," I said breathlessly, and we kissed again and I clung to him and felt wonderful and terrible at the same time. Star-crossed lovers. What would happen to us? And what would Amber do if she knew?

I saw Paul later on that night. He and I had zeroed out, though. We had absolutely nothing to say to each other that was worth saying, and he was acting

like a kid, messing around tickling me and pretending
to hide my purse, sticking it down his trousers and
asking me to look for it.

As if, I thought. I knew his game all right.

He was just so immature compared to Mac.
I couldn't think what I'd ever seen in him.

When he walked me home he asked me if he was
coming in for a coffee.

"I don't think so," I said. "I want an early night."
I just wanted to go indoors and dream about Mac.
To hold tight to my pillow and pretend it was him.

"Aw, come on," he said. He put his arms round me
and I wriggled away. "What's wrong with you?" he
asked.

"Nothing. I'm just not in the mood," I said irritably.

His eyes narrowed. "And...?"

"And – well, I think I've gone off you," I said, which sounds a bit drastic, but at least it was truthful. I never believe in pussyfooting around where boys are concerned. Either you go out with them, or you don't. I don't like playing games.

His eyes widened and he pulled a sneery face. "Get you!"

"Sorry," I said. "I just ... I think we've been seeing each other long enough. No strings, we said. We don't want to be a drag to each other, do we?"

There was a moment's silence, then he said, "Found someone else, have you? Who is he?"

I shook my head. "No. There's no one."

"Not yet."

"No. Not yet," I said, and went indoors.

I did think of writing a bit more of the letter, but in the end I didn't. It would waste precious dreaming-about-Mac time.

Chapter Five

I couldn't wait for Saturday. Just couldn't wait.
I pictured it in my head: where we'd meet, how he'd
look, what he'd say to me. I imagined us sitting
nibbling at our food, all loved-up, unable to eat.
He'd hold my hand under the table and we'd look
into each other's eyes and I'd know for sure that this
was the real thing.

I'd had loads of boyfriends, but I hadn't had loads
of romance. This time it was going to be different. It
would be just like in the books and movies.

I felt awful about Amber, of course – it was such a mess. Not only did I feel guilty, but I was as jealous as hell of anything she said about Mac. We were all at Jo's house on Tuesday and we were talking about boys and Amber started saying how lovely Mac was, and how generous, and how he said the nicest things. When she said *that* I felt so choked up with jealousy that I could hardly speak.

"What sort of things?" I heard myself asking.

"Oh, just that he's been thinking of me during the day, and missing me. And he said that he looks at my star sign in the newspaper every day."

"He's got it bad!" Jo said. "Guys don't usually do that."

"Yesterday he said that it would be brilliant if we

could go away together for the weekend. He's got relatives in Scotland and he wants to take me there."

"Really?" I said. I plastered a bright smile on my face, but inside my tummy turned over. Was she speaking the truth? Why had he said that to her if he was going to end it between them?

"I wish you could all find someone as brilliant as he is!" she said suddenly, and I thought to myself, I have...

A bit later Nicki and I walked back from Jo's together and I brought up the subject of Mac and Amber.

"What d'you think?" I asked. "Is he for real?"

Nicki shrugged. "Dunno. Sounds a bit too good to be true, I reckon."

"That's what I thought," I said. Fishing for more, I added, "I'm just not sure about him."

"I reckon she's keener than he is."

"Do you?" I asked eagerly.

"Well, she never stops going on about him – but I bet he's not always going on about her. Well, you never have boys getting all loved-up about a girl, do you?"

I shook my head. "Not like they get about football."

"It's like when Jo was going out with that boy she met on holiday. That Vince bloke. She went on about him twenty-four-seven and then when it came to it – well, I don't reckon he ever existed."

But I wasn't interested in talking about Jo and Vince. "So, you don't think it'll last between Mac and Amber?"

She looked at me strangely. "What d'you want to know for?"

"Just want to be ready with the tissues," I said.

"Oh yeah?" As I said, we've all been friends a long time – and Nicki probably knows me better than the others. "Fancy him yourself, do you?"

"Nah," I said, "not really. Though he is pretty fit."

"You're telling me!" she said. "*Phworr!*"

I laughed, my insides doing cartwheels. Nicki felt it too: Mac was a guy and a half. And he was going to be mine – all mine.

When I got in Mum was home, sitting in the study with a pile of papers. She said that Paul had rung.

"He wanted to talk to you and he sounded quite stressed out," she said. "I told him you'd ring back tonight."

I groaned. "I've given him the push," I said. "I don't want to go through it all again now. I'll ring him in a couple of days."

"Tonight," she said firmly. "I promised."

She practically frog-marched me into the hall and made me dial his number, then went back into the study.

I thought I'd let the phone ring a couple of times and then put the receiver down and tell Mum he wasn't in, but he answered on the first ring. He started going on at me – he'd obviously been thinking about it all day.

"You've got someone else, haven't you? I bet you've been two-timing me. Who is it?"

"I *haven't* got anyone else," I said. Well, that was true at the moment.

"Just tell me his name. Is it someone from round here?"

"I haven't *got* anyone," I repeated, getting ratty now. "I'd tell you *if* I had. The reason we're not seeing each other any more is that I think we've gone on long enough. That's all."

"Look, give me another chance, right? That's all I want. We can—"

"Look, I'm really sorry, Paul," I interrupted, "but when it's over – it's over."

"Who *is* it you're seeing? Tell me!"

"I keep telling you – I'm not seeing anyone. And I'm going to bed now. Goodnight!"

I put the receiver down and then I picked it up again and left it off the hook, in case he rang back.

I went upstairs to get ready for bed, thinking deeply as I cleaned my teeth and took off my make-up. Mac and I would obviously have to keep things quiet for a while. Once he'd told Amber that it was over between them, I'd leave it at least a couple of weeks – maybe longer – before announcing that we were an item. Paul would get over it, of course. Amber, too. Well, I hoped she would...

Chapter Six

For various reasons – Jo was going to her granny's
with her sister, Nicki had to go out with her mum –
the four of us weren't meeting to go shopping on
Saturday.

I was *so* relieved. How would I have faced Amber,
knowing that I was going out with her boyfriend that
very night? As it was, she'd already told me that she
wouldn't be seeing him that evening. "He's got
relatives coming down from Scotland," she said, and
I'd turned away, feeling myself go red.

How could I do such a thing?

I asked myself this a hundred times, and managed to come up with "I can't help myself" and "I didn't mean it to happen". I didn't think either of them were much of an excuse, but they were all I could think of.

Would Amber – or any of the others – do the same to me? Would they accept a date with one of their best friends' boyfriends? The answer was: they would if they were mad about him – as mad as I was about Mac. I was sure they would.

I got out my letter to Liz. I hadn't sent it and I knew why: I thought she'd say that I was doing something terrible and tell me to stop. I'd read replies to girls on her page before and she was quite sarcastic if they were doing the dirty on their best mates. "Great friend *you're* turning out to be" she'd said once, and "With friends like you, who needs enemies?"

If she said that to me I'd feel even worse.

I did a little timetable for myself and tried to put thoughts of Amber to the back of my mind. I was meeting Mac in town – at the arcade – at seven-thirty, and he'd told me (a snatched conversation by the lockers on Thursday) that he was going to book a table in one of the Italian restaurants. So ... I calculated rapidly ... if I worked on my school project in the morning, then I could devote the whole afternoon to getting ready and catch the bus into town at ten past seven.

Getting ready for a first date, a very special date, is almost as fun as the date itself. That afternoon I borrowed all Mum's expensive beauty spa treatments and spent hours in the bathroom, playing sloppy love songs on my CD player while I soaked and conditioned and manicured and mudpacked every bit of me. Then I very carefully made up my face. Mum (who was out, as usual) had once paid for me to have a make-up lesson. I got out all the stuff I'd been persuaded to buy and tried to remember what I'd been taught.

I was ready and dressed by six o'clock. I had on an expensive, very short, black dress that Mum had bought me to meet some of her clients in, and I dowsed myself in her million-pound-a-millilitre (or so she said) perfume.

I surveyed the finished effect: I looked about eighteen. And – well, even if I say so myself – pretty good, actually. I imagined Mac seeing me, imagined him looking me up and down, eyes flickering over me, smiling in appreciation.

I walked into the sitting-room, and as I did so the phone started ringing. I dashed back into the hall to answer it, but then, just as I reached it, decided to leave it. If it was Mac to say the date was off, I didn't want to know; I'd rather go into town and take my chances. If it was Nicki or one of the others wanting to see me that night – well, I obviously couldn't go, and I didn't want to make up any more lies. If it was one of Mum's clients (and it usually was) then they could wait until tomorrow.

The phone stopped and I breathed again. It was bound to be one of Mum's clients, I told myself. They rang her day and night. I didn't check, though.

I went back into the sitting-room, flicked on the TV and started watching a game show. I couldn't concentrate, though. I was all knotted up inside and felt almost sick. What was wrong with me? It must be love – I'd never felt so peculiar before.

At six forty-five exactly, the front doorbell rang and I nearly jumped out of my skin. Horrified, I just sat there, not moving.

It rang again, longer and more insistent, so I got up, tiptoed into our front dining-room and peered out through a crack in the venetian blind. Maybe it was Mac, come to collect me.

I looked out. It wasn't Mac.

It was Amber.

And she'd seen the blind move, because she looked directly at me and waved her hand. Her hair was scraped back from her face, her face was blotchy – she'd obviously been crying.

I dropped the edge of the blind, my heart pounding like a drum. What on earth was I going to do now? I couldn't leave her on the doorstep; she knew I was in.

What did she want? Had she somehow found out about me and Mac?

The bell rang again and slowly, hesitantly, I went to the door and opened it.

Amber burst into tears at the sight of me. "Oh, Zoe!" she said, not seeming to notice that I was all dressed up. "I tried to ring. I've got to talk to you! It's about Mac..."

I gulped. Did she know or not? Was she just biding her time? "Well, I ... er ... I might be going out soon. But come in anyway."

She wiped her nose on her sleeve and I went to get her some tissues from the downstairs cloakroom. I feared the very worst.

I handed over a wodge of tissues with a hand that was shaking. "Come and sit down," I said. "What's the matter?"

We sat on the sofa and she cried for some minutes – big sobs so that she couldn't speak. I just sat there, watching her, patting her arm. Did she know or didn't she know?

After a few moments she calmed down and blew her nose. Then she said shakily, "Mac's got someone else."

My heart plummeted. He'd told her already!

What was I going to say now? What lies could I make up? "Really?" I managed to ask. "Are you sure?"

She nodded.

I swallowed. "But how...?"

"I ... I went round this afternoon. I wasn't seeing him tonight and I wanted to get back a school-book I'd lent him. His mum answered the door and she said he was out." She gave another sob.

"And?" I prompted after a moment.

"I said who I was and his mum looked at me really strangely – as if she'd never heard of me. And then she said, 'I'm afraid he's out with his girlfriend, dear.'"

I looked at Amber in horror. I was devastated. Of course I felt sorry for her, but – selfish only child that I am – sorrier still for myself. "No!"

Amber nodded. "I know who it is, too."

I froze. Absolutely froze.

"It's a girl called Jessica," Amber said. "*Jessica*. What a bloody stupid name."

Relief rushed over me and I suddenly felt as weak as a kitten. Thank God she didn't know about me! "Wonder what she's like?" I mumbled. "Do we know a Jessica?"

Amber shook her head. "His mum said he's been

going out with her since the summer – when they moved down here. She's a year older than him and lives in the flats at the end of his road."

"Oh," I said. I could hardly believe it: he wasn't just two-timing Amber, he was two-timing me as well! I'd thought he was different – more thoughtful, more mature, more genuine than the other guys. And all the time...

"What're you going to do now?" I asked.

Amber shrugged. "Give him the elbow, of course. Before he gives it to me. I'm going to write him a stinker of a letter." She suddenly seemed to see me for the first time. "Hey, look at you all dressed up! Where're you going?"

I swallowed. "Nowhere," I said. "Just ... just trying

out some make-up." I gave her a half-smile. "If you like," I said, "I'll help you write to him."

She only hesitated a moment. "That'd be great," she said. "Thanks. But are you sure you aren't going anywhere?"

I shook my head slowly. "Nowhere at all," I said, and I went upstairs to get my notepad. I hated, really *hated* Mac for what he'd done, and for what he'd nearly made me do to Amber. The letter to Liz wouldn't get finished – but now I'd be helping Amber write a very different kind of letter...

Find out what Amber, Jo, Nicki and Zoe get up to

in another book from the Letters to Liz series:

Amber's Letter

(Turn the page to read the first chapter.)

Chapter One

It was the night I went to the cinema with my mates, Zoe, Nicki and Jo, that I first suspected something was going on. It was Friday and we'd been to the multiplex in town to see this film about people having affairs. It was supposed to be a comedy, and basically everyone was copping off with everyone else's boyfriend or girlfriend, husband or wife. None of the relationships were what they seemed. The film was OK, but not brilliant. The good thing was that it hadn't cost us anything because Zoe's mum had got us free tickets.

The four of us are really close friends and we go round together all the time. Sometimes – when one of us is going out with a boy and it's getting all smoochy – we don't see as much of each other as usual, but in the end it always comes back to us four: best friends for ever.

Mum was out when I got home from the cinema that night. This wasn't unusual for a Friday because she goes to a book group where they have long discussions about what they're reading. Afterwards they sometimes go on to a pub for a meal. Dad was home, though, because he was looking after my little brother Liam, who's seven. I've also got an older brother, Aidan, but he'd gone on a month-long course with his catering college.

Liam was in bed and Dad was in the sitting-room when I let myself in. Our front door is new and doesn't squeak when you open or close it, so although I said hello to Dad, the TV was on and he obviously hadn't heard me. I stood in the hall taking my jacket off and was just about to give Dad a yell when the music on the TV died down. I realized he was on the phone.

He was laughing – giggling, in fact. And this was rare. I mean, I have heard him giggle about things but not for ages. And certainly not with Mum. Bickering – yes. Giggling – no. And when he stopped giggling he said in a low voice, "Oh, you kill me, you know that?"

I hesitated outside the door for a moment, hearing him say that and thinking how strange it sounded. I mean, I couldn't think of anyone he would say that to. He just didn't have friends like that. And then almost immediately I started thinking about the film I'd just seen – the film about affairs. It was the sort of way they'd spoken to each other in that: in a joky, flattering, warm way.

I held my breath, listening.

"OK, Chicky," he went on. "Let's decide what time on Sunday and—"

But I'd heard enough. I was scared of what I'd hear next. Before he could say anything else I barged in. "Hi!" I said. "What's on telly?"

Chicky was the name he called me sometimes, and

called my little brother too, when he was in a good mood. Chicky meaning chicken, because he said we had browny-gold hair exactly the same colour as a chicken's feathers. But who was he calling that now?

Dad looked up, startled. "Amber! Just a sec," he said. He spoke into the receiver in a different voice. "See you soon, all right? Bye now!" He put the phone down.

"Who was that?" I asked.

"Bloke from work," he said. He kept his head down and didn't look at me. Rummaging through the newspapers on the floor he found that day's TV programmes. "Now, what have we got on next?" he muttered.

I stared at him. Bloke from work indeed! I didn't

believe him. You didn't call blokes from work Chicky.
I thought about the film I'd just seen. Everyone had
been at it in that – shop girls and office workers,
teenagers and married women, the doctor and the
secretary. They were all having affairs. And now –
well, it seemed like my dad might be having one
too.

I didn't sleep very well that night – I was too
worried. Was he having an affair? Was it serious? What
was going to happen next? Would he and Mum be
getting a divorce? I wished there was someone I
could tell. If Aidan had been home I could have
talked to him about it, but he would be away for
three more weeks.

*   *   *

The following morning my new copy of *Sue CQ*, the teen magazine, arrived, and I read it in bed, looking for features about people having affairs. Was it really as common as that film was trying to make out? Was everyone at it? How could you find out if they were?

I read the mag from cover to cover but I couldn't find anything about affairs, just the usual quizzes and fashion, and stuff about boy bands. There weren't even any problems about two-timing on the *Letters to Liz* problem pages.

I got up about eleven, still feeling worried, had a shower and went downstairs. Liam was riding his bike round and round the garden and Mum and Dad were eating bacon sandwiches in the kitchen. They were arguing, as usual. Dad was saying that he liked his bacon crispier and that the bread always went soggy the way *she* made sandwiches, and Mum was saying that if he was so bloody fussy he could make them himself.

I flopped down at the table, sighing loudly. "Give it a rest," I said. "Do you have to row every single day?"

Mum looked at me in surprise. "We're not rowing, Amber," she said, "just having a discussion."

"Sounds like a row to me," I said.

I stared at Dad. Did he look different? The men in the film all had new haircuts, shirts or shoes when they were having affairs. They'd started wearing aftershave and using new shampoos, and one had even had his hair tinted. Dad always looked pretty good, I thought. He didn't have a paunch, like most men his age, and he kept his hair nice and short and wore quite trendy clothes. At least he didn't wear patterned golfing jumpers like Nicki's dad.

"What are you staring at?" he suddenly asked me.

"Nothing!" I looked away and my glance fell on Mum. She looked a bit of a sight, actually. She was wearing jogging trousers and an old T-shirt of mine which had something spilt down the front. Her hair – which used to be goldie-brown like mine and my brother's – had been permed so many times it looked dry and straw-like.

Perhaps that was why Dad... But as soon as I thought that I pushed the idea away. Just because Mum had let herself go a bit didn't give Dad the right to have an affair. If he *was* having an affair.

I finished my cereal and Dad and Mum had coffee. Dad made it, then he said it tasted bitter and asked Mum if she'd bought the cheap brand. She said she'd bought the first ground coffee she'd seen – she didn't have time to pick and choose – but if he wanted to take over the shopping himself he was quite welcome ... blah ... blah ... blah. And so it went on.

I was just about to get myself round to Jo's house – the four of us were meeting up and going shopping, as we usually did on a Saturday – when Dad said something about not being here the next day. He said he had to go into work to do the end-of-year accounts. Mum just shrugged as if she couldn't care less, but I looked at him suspiciously, remembering what he'd said on the phone the night before.

"Going to work on a *Sunday*?" I said. "I don't remember you ever doing that before."

"I've never been so behind with the accounts before," he said.

I fixed him with a look. I bet I know what you're up to, I thought...